more

MISSING PIECES

Her Story
of Irish Women

First published in 1985 by
ATTIC PRESS
(in conjunction with Women in Community Publishing Course 1984/85)
48 Fleet Street,
Dublin 2.

More missing pieces: her story of Irish women.
  1. Women — Ireland — Biography
  I. Caherty, Therese   II. MacConville, Catherine. III. Dixon, Patricia
  920.72'09415   CT365017

  ISBN 0-946211-17-5

Typeset in 10pt Baskerville by Photoset Ltd.
Printed in Ireland by Mount Salus Press.

EDITORIAL/PRODUCTION: Therese Caherty
COVER DESIGN AND ILLUSTRATION: Catherine MacConville
RESEARCH: Therese Caherty, Rita Corley, Patricia Dixon, Catherine MacConville

more MISSING PIECES

Her Story of Irish Women

Attic Press, Dublin.

ACKNOWLEDGEMENTS

We gratefully acknowledge the assistance of: Louise Barry, Arlen House; Frank Bissett, NCAD; Patricia Boylan, United Arts Club; Finbar Boyle, Dept. of Irish Folklore; Clodagh Boyd; Declan Bree; Kieran Burke, Cork City Library; Geraldine Carroll; Pat Carroll, WIP; Mary Clarke, Archives Division City Hall; Mai Clifford, IWWU; Ned Comerford, Kytelers of Kilkenny; Cork Examiner; Michael Costeloe, Commissioners of Irish Lights; Constance Cowley; Rosemary Cullen Owens; Gaye Cunningham; Tony Dawson, Cork and Kerry Tourism; Angela de Búrca, UCD; John de Courcy Ireland; Siobhan de hÓir, Royal Society of Antiquaries of Ireland; Maurice Dockrell; Ursula Dooley; Alan Figgis; Mr Fitzmaurice; Shielah Flitton; Jude Flynn, Longford Historical Society; Margaret Gaj; Cathal Goan, RTE Dublin; Nóirín Greene; Myra Hick née Considine; Irish Independent; Irish Press; Irish Times; Pauline Jackson, Women's Studies Forum UCD; Margaret Jennings, Roscommon Champion; Máirín Johnston; Mary Jones, IWWU Archives; Marion Keaney, Leabharlann Chontae Longfoirt-Iarmhí; Eillen Kennedy; Prof. Colm Kiernan, Dept. of History UCD; Helen Kilcline, Roscommon County Library; Helen Lanigan Wood, Curator of Fermanagh County Museum; Michael Ledwith; Dorothy Leonard; Rhoda MacManus, Hawkswell Theatre Sligo; Patsy Murphy, College of Commerce Rathmines; National Gallery of Ireland; National Monuments Branch, Commissioners of Public Works; Anna Ní Dhómhnaill; Máiréad Ní Dhómhnaill; Robert Nicholson, Curator of the Joyce Tower Sandycove; David Norris; Olive Nugent; Piaras O'Connor; Mrs O'Cuiv; Molly O'Duffy; Aidan O'Hare; Sean Ó'Suilleabháin, Leitrim County Library; Jeff Palmer; Hallie Quinlan; Mary Quinlan; Lorna Reynolds; Jean Roche, Communist Party of Ireland; Sue Russell; Margaret Shanahan, Daisy Swanton; Anne Tannahill, Blackstaff Press; Kathleen Taylor; Martin A. Timoney, Sligo Field Club; Ríonach Uí Ógáin, Dept. of Irish Folklore UCD; Catherine Whitney; Bridie Whoriskey, RTE Galway.

A very special thanks to all those people who responded to our letters — their material will be used in Missing Pieces 1986!

Special thanks to Anne Claffey for her editorial assistance.

Special thanks also to Pat Caherty; Roisin Conroy, IFI; Monica Cullinane, Library UCD; Moira Dolan, IFI; Mary Paul Keane, Attic Press; Patricia Kelleher, IFI; Anne O'Connor, Dept. of Irish Folklore UCD; and all the women on the Women in Community Publishing Course for their good humour and support at all times.

CONTENTS

ILLUSTRATIONS

INTRODUCTION

Since women have always been written out of our heritage, the purpose of *More Missing Pieces* is to write them straight back in. This sequel to *Missing Pieces Volume 1* unfolds a rich patchwork of Irish life in which women's roles are celebrated and restored to their rightful place in our culture.

It became evident through research that women's exploits and activities were varied and far reaching. They ranged from the exotic to the practical; from pirating in the Caribbean to campaigning for more suitable school lunch hours for mothers. In all instances they reflect a courage, an excitement and a humour that demands attention and recognition.

Frequently documentation concerning individuals was too scanty to be of any real value and further sources of information proved impossible to locate. It is in this respect that you, the reader, can participate in the recording of her story of Irish women. By retrieving the fragments of information still existent in oral tradition, the lives of many women who have been buried in that tradition, will be rediscovered and so enrich our understanding of our past.

The *Women in Community Publishing Course*, funded jointly by AnCO and the European Social Fund and run by Irish Feminist Information undertook this particular project with several aims in mind. We intended these biographies to be concise. They were designed to introduce the reader to such well known characters as Grace O'Malley, the Mayo pirate, alongside lesser known individuals such as Molly O'Reilly who in 1916 hoisted the old Irish flag over Liberty Hall. In compiling *More Missing Pieces* we wished to stimulate interest, and thereby encourage research, in this much neglected area.

The cover design of *More Missing Pieces* is based on a patchwork quilt designed and sewn in Ulster in the nineteenth century. Investigation into the distinctive characteristics of Irish patchwork reveals that it was an implicit part of a woman's work. So this craft illustrates another area specifically belonging to women, an area rich in tradition and artistry yet unforgiveably ignored up until quite recently.

Missing Pieces Volume 1 began the work of liberating women from the chains of obscurity, throwing light on their contributions to our lives. *More Missing Pieces* continues this delving into our past and with your help will uncover more women who deserve a place in our story books.

April 1985

LILY ANDERSON
1922-1982

Despite widespread prejudice in Belfast, 'nursery schools are for lazy mothers', Lily Anderson became a pioneer in changing public opinion so that nursery schools became a priority and not a luxury.

She was one of the mothers who used the war-time nursery centres in Belfast, and in particular Oakmount Drive Nursery. It closed in the late 1940s and the children moved to Frederick Street Nursery School. Attached to it was a Mothers' Club which joined forces with other similar clubs to form the Nursery Mothers' Action Campaign of 1964-66. Lily was a vital force in this campaign, pointing out that under the 1947 Education Act, nursery schools were supposed to be provided where

there was a demand. The educational value of the nurseries was stressed, along with the traffic hazards to small children in built up inner city areas with no playgrounds and the health of the mothers confined to high rise flats with young children. The campaign was a success, two new nursery schools were opened in the New Lodge and Victoria Barrack Estate. Other schools were promised, and though slow in materialising, were provided by the mid seventies.

Lily became a member of the Communist Party in 1942 and for many years served on its sub-committees for Education, Social Services and Women. She died tragically in Bulgaria in August 1981, from a fall off a bus.

Lily Anderson.

NORA BARNACLE
1884-1951

When pushed to the limits of endurance, Nora Barnacle threatened to baptise her children if James Joyce did not give up the drink! An extraordinary woman who completed her formal education at thirteen, Nora was brought up a Galway catholic. It is speculated that she abandoned her religion when a liaison with a protestant, Willy Mulvagh, was frowned upon by her family. The consequences of their disapproval was her exile to Dublin, where, alone and aged twenty, she got herself a job in Finn's Hotel in Leinster Street, off Nassau Street. It was here that she met and formed the unorthodox alliance with James Joyce. The decision to embark on a 'hazardous life' with him was hers and hers alone, despite the fact that she was still a minor and that Joyce's highbrow friends thought her beneath him. She flouted tradition and set sail with him for Trieste in 1904.

In Europe the Barnacle-Joyce odyssey began, one of poverty and often misery. Nora had little or no time for Joyce's work, offering to sell the first edition of *Ulysses*, refusing to read it and ultimately declaring that 'Jim should have stuck to the singing and not bothered with the writing'. With no second language, and no desire to learn one, her life was bleak and bare and her companion did not help by drinking any spare money they had. She had two children, Giorgio born in July 1905, and Lucia Anna in July 1907 (who was born, like Nora, in a paupers' ward). She did not marry Joyce until she was forty seven. Her imaginative turn of phrase and forthrightness were a breath of fresh air in the literary circles in which she moved.

Nora Barnacle.

Nora Barnacle died in Zurich 10 April 1951, aged 67. She had suffered severely from arthritis and the massive does of cortisone which she took for her condition brought on uremic poisoning.

MARGARET BARRINGTON 1896-1982

Margaret Barrington, an exceptional and prolific writer, died on 8 March 1982 just five months before her first collection of short stories, *David's Daughter, Tamar* was published. For more than thirty years she had lived in almost total obscurity and isolation in West Cork — forgotten as a writer. Shortly before her death, symbolically coinciding with International Women's Day, her life's work unfolded through the discovery of a wealth of unpublished material which had lain dormant for decades seen only up to this time by herself. A selection was passed onto a publisher, who, ironically, had rediscovered the books of her second husband Liam O'Flaherty, from whom she separated in 1932.

The acclaim for which she had waited so long came too late — an acclaim she had touched upon with the publication of her first and only novel,

My Cousin Justin, which at its time of publication in 1939 was received with great enthusiasm by the critics.

Margaret Barrington's life, from her birth in Malin, County Donegal in 1896, through her two marriages, her political activities, which include helping refugees to escape from Nazi Germany and most of all her writings will be remembered, because Margaret Barrington has left us something worthwhile to remind us of her.

KATTY BARRY
c. 1900-1982

In Katty Barry's famous eating house people sat about the bubbling pot or cauldron, flames flickering underneath, yarning and singing until well into the small hours. They fortified themselves with port, cider, wine and crubeens and were entertained with their own songs and lively conversations.

Katty Barry's was established by her mother and business was carried on there well into the sixties. In the old days it catered for the market gardeners coming early to town to sell their produce. When Katty, radiating life and vitality, took it over, the people came from far and wide. A woman of outrageous wit and humour, she was choosey about her clientele, refusing admittance to those whose appearance did not please her. She had a dealer's respect for money but this did not prevent her from being generous to those in need and often credentials did in lieu of a purse.

She loved a wide range of music,

including nationalist songs and romantic operettas. Deeply religious, she never neglected the red lamp before the picture of the Sacred Heart. The stuff of legends clings still to Katty Barry, a figure well-known in verse and song in her native Cork. She died after a long illness in 1982.

Katty Barry.

KATHLEEN BEHAN nee KEARNEY
c. 1889-1984

'If there is a heaven, it must be for working women,' said Kathleen Behan. At ninety, she released her first long-playing record and at ninety-five she saw the publication of her autobiography *Mother of all the Behans*. She lived a long and varied life, the secret of which she said was 'good humour, singing and dancing, and jumping around in general'.

Born in Capel Street, North Dublin, in 1889, she was removed from the family at the age of nine and put into Goldenbridge Orphanage when they hit hard times — 'a dull, cold place to go on a dull, cold day'. It was here she developed her life-long interest in reading.

During the Easter Rising she carried messages to Padraig Pearse and James Connolly. Her first husband Jack Furlong died during the great 'flu epidemic of 1918 and Kathleen was left with one son and another on the way. Soon after the birth of her second son, Constance Markievicz got her a job in Maud Gonne MacBride's house on St Stephen's Green. It was here that she met Sarah Purser, who painted her portrait now hanging in the National Gallery.

In 1922 she set up house with Stephen Behan but when he became a prisoner of the Free State for two years Kathleen was obliged to move from slum to slum during that time. There were five children to this marriage and, although times were very hard, family life for the Behans was full of

Kathleen Behan from a painting by Sarah Purser.

lively conversation, books, music and a strong sense of Irish cultural tradition.

The 1940s were dominated for her by the political and other escapades of her sons, Brendan and Dominick. In the 1970s Kathleen appeared on TV chat shows on the BBC and RTE. 'A fierce feminist and republican (old IRA)', was how daughter-in-law, Beatrice, described her. Kathleen died in 1984.

GEORGE ANNE BELLAMY
c. 1733-1788

Although her last years were spent in poverty and obscurity, George Anne Bellamy caused a sensation in 1785 when she published her *Apology,* a six volume account of her tempestuous career in the theatre. Beautiful, proud, twice married, once bigamously, she was one of David Garrick's leading actresses, her first appearance in Covent Garden in 1744 assuring her of acclaim.

Born in Fingal, County Dublin on St George's Day, 23 April c. 1733, her name was a corruption of Georgiana probably misheard at the christening. She returned to Dublin in 1760 after her London career and was a tremendous success but her fame diminished with the years and by 1780 Dublin no longer saluted her. She retired in 1785 and Covent Garden organised a benefit in her honour. She was a good friend to the Gunning Sisters, helping them out in times of financial difficulty and introducing them to many of her influential contacts. As with a lot of people of strong temperament, George

Anne attracted a good deal of antipathy and her compatriot, Peg Woffington, attacked her once, and stabbed her. She died on 10 February 1788.

LADY BETTY
c. 1750-1810

A woman of 'dark disposition' was the Lady Betty, whose son was the only source of comfort in her bleak existence. Widowed early in life and crushed by bitter, hopeless poverty her son set sail for America and its promise of gold. Eventually, his letters home to Kerry ceased and his mother gave him up for dead, continuing a life made more desolate by his loss. Some years later, so the story goes, a strange man required lodgings in her house and taunted the miserable Betty with tales

The Old Jail, Roscommon.

Anne Bonney with her friend Mary Read.

of his immense wealth. Seizing her opportunity, she murdered him in the night and, too late, discovered his identity. It was her long-lost son, whose perverse sense of humour had been his undoing.

Betty was wretched and the cause of her misery was soon public knowledge. She was sentenced to hang, but on the appointed day there was no executioner. She promptly volunteered for the job, thus gaining clemency, and carried out the executions, unmasked and undisguised. In later years she developed a habit of drawing with a burnt stick on the walls of her apartment, the portraits of the people she had executed. So the luckless woman became the Lady Betty, Finisher of the Law for the Connaught Circuit, in particular Roscommon, for many years.

ANNE BONNEY
18th Century

'If he had fought like a man he need not have been hanged like a dog,' said the imprisoned Anne Bonney when asked if she wanted to see Captain Jack Rackham (Calico Jack), a fellow pirate before his death.

Born in Cork in 1700, she went with her father to Charleston, South Carolina while still young. A teenager with a remarkable temperament, she is said to have murdered her English maid and married a worthless fellow without her father's consent. Inevitably she was cast out of home and later abandoned by her new husband.

But her fortitude and stubborness saw her through. Alone in the docks area she encountered Calico Jack, whose tales of daring and adventure captured her imagination. Enthralled by the notion of piracy she boarded his ship disguised as a man and there met her notorious companion Mary Read, also disguised. Before long, Anne had developed a more than passing interest for Mary and only then revealed her true sex to her. Together the two sailed the Caribbean, and the crew said that there was no one aboard more resolute in times of battle than they.

When captured and tried for piracy in 1720, both women said they were pregnant in order to evade hanging. Calico Jack was not so lucky. Mary unfortunately died in prison and Anne was the only one to survive. Grenada issued a stamp in her memory in 1970.

ELLEN BUSHELL
1880-1948

The Abbey Theatre, Dublin was surrounded by British Black and Tan soldiers. Inside Michael Collins sat, unaware of the danger he was in. Someone informed the young attendant of what was happening and she immediately went to Collins and helped him to exit safely into a hidden laneway.

Ellen Bushell or Nellie, as she was known, worked in the Abbey for forty-three years and was on the original staff when it opened on 27 December 1904. Yet, strange as it may seem, Lennox Robinson's written account of the Abbey Theatre up to 1952 omits even a mention of one who was as much a part of its tradition as the famous Abbey gong.

Born in Dublin in 1880, her father was a silk weaver of Huguenot extraction and one of her hobbies was poplin weaving from threads of her own spinning. During the War of Independence she was a member of Collins' intelligence and her house in Inchicore was often used as a shelter for men on the run. She was also a collector of lore, one of her prized possessions being a manuscript copy of *The Soldier's Song* which she took down on the night it was composed. After the show it was customary for Nellie and her friends to walk to her home and have a 'pow-wow', as she described it. They talked for hours, reviving themselves with sausages, pudding and stout. It was in this atmosphere that Nellie first heard and copied down the National Anthem.

In 1948 she was buried with full military honours at Mount Jerome Cemetery and was awarded the 1916 medal and the War of Independence medal with active service bar.

ANNE CLANCY
1698-c.1750

Born April 1, 1698, Anne Clancy was the first known woman to set sail around the world. She set out on 7 September 1718 in her twenty foot curragh, built with her own hands. Her diaries tell of an incredibly harrowing and difficult journey. Her many encounters with storms and other sea dangers prepared Anne for her eventual encounter with pirates.

Joining the pirate ship *El Cazador* she continued her journey and eventually

arrived at her destination Tierra del
Fuego, South America.

Her last adventure was a river journey
up the Amazon. No conclusive
documentary evidence details her
return and folk memory of the area tells
of a great white goddess who lived with
her people for many years and was
known as 'The Mother of the People'.

The bulk of Anne's diaries detailing this
unique adventure have unfortunately
been lost and the few remaining pages
give us only a taste of one of the most
unusual women in Irish herstory.

FRANCES POWER COBBE *c.* 1822-1904

After moving to England, following
the death of her father for whom she
had kept house, Frances Power Cobbe,
taught in Mary Carpenter's 'Ragged
Schools' (for the poorest children) in
Bristol. She began to write at the age of
forty as a means of campaigning for
various social reforms. In one instance
she successfully pleaded for the release
of a woman who had killed her
husband in self-defence and had been
sentenced to hang. Her feminist work
included initiating legislation which
empowered women to legally separate
from violent husbands and to retain
custody of their children.

As a young woman in County Dublin,
daughter of Anglo-Irish aristocrats,
she began to cultivate radical ideas
about society and religion. Her closest
friend there, Harriet St Léger, was
another rebel, famous for wearing for-
bidden clothes — trousers!

Frances Power Cobbe.

On her travels abroad Frances met the
sculptor, Mary Lloyd. They lived
together for many years in Hereford
Square, South Kensington, London,
before retiring to Wales, where they
were finally buried together at
Hengwrt, near Barmouth.

In her lifetime Frances was
enormously respected and loved for
her efforts on behalf of higher
education for women; as a campaigner
for workhouse reforms; as a teacher in
the 'Ragged Schools'; as a writer of
treatises on ethics; and as a tireless
worker in the anti-vivisection movement. Frances lived a life of remarkable achievement.

MARY MARGARET COLUM
1894-1957

Mary Margaret Colum was born in Colloney, County Sligo. She was the daughter of Maria Gunning, a descendant of the famous Gunning sisters, and Charles Maguire.

Mary Margaret Colum taught in a school founded by Pearse and wrote a pamphlet, *St. Enda's School Rathfarnham*, in 1918 on her experience there. She was a regular visitor to The Abbey Theatre and was involved in the literary revival spearheaded by George Russell, Yeats and Synge. Here she met Lady Gregory, Maude Gonne, Constance Markievicz, George Sigerson and Sarah Purser.

She contributed to *The Irish Review* founded by Padraic Colum whom she married in 1912. During her time in New York she established herself as a well known literary critic and member of The Poetry Society. She contributed to *Dial, Scribner's Magazine, The Freemam* and from 1934-1940 she was literary art critic for *Forum and Century,* and a widely recognised authority on French poetry.

In 1930 and 1938 she received the Guggenheim Fellowship in literary criticism and in 1934 Georgestown University awarded her its John Ryder gold metal for distinction in Literature. She was elected to the National Institute of Arts and Letters in 1953.

Her autobiography *Life and Dreams* appeared in 1947, an outstanding success running into several editions.

Mary Margaret Column died in New York in October 1957. Her body was brought back to Ireland and buried in St Fintan's Cemetery, Sutton, County Dublin.

MIA CRANWILL
c. 1880-1972

Years of work with difficult metals took their toll on Mia Cranwill, who in her late sixties was advised to leave her work as a designer in metals as there was a danger of her losing the use of both arms. At this time she took to weaving her own designs on a small hand-loom and, at the age of seventy,

Christmas Card design by Mia Cranwill.

did black and white illustrations for Dolmen Press.

She had a wealth of work to her credit, her greatest achievement and personal memorial being the tabernacle, sanctuary lamp and benediction monstrance which she created for St. Patrick's Church in San Francisco. The monstrance took two years, and the tabernacle four, to complete. She took the tabernacle herself to Liverpool to ensure its safe passage to San Francisco. Unique Celtic touches were introduced into each piece, such as the ancient Irish technique of getting colour contrast by the use of different metals.

She always claimed to be a Wexford woman, although she was born in north Dublin in March 1880. At fifteen she moved with her family to England, where she studied art in Salford and Manchester School of Art. But a deep-seated longing to live and work in Dublin brought her back in 1917. She set up workshops, first in Suffolk Street, Dublin, over a bicycle shop, and later in Killiney. She received many commissions, among them one from Count McCormack, who wanted a pectoral cross similar to the Cross of Cong in Mayo. She also made the episcopal ring for the Bishop of Clonfert. The army requested her to design the standards for the First, Second and Fourth Brigades. They were each to have a theme which would be of particular significance to the brigade to which they were assigned.

Although busy and mentally alert, she spent the final ten years of her life at Alexandra Guild House. Once dubbed the Benvenuto Cellini* of Ireland, Mia Cranwill died 20 October 1972.

* *A famous sixteenth century Venetian goldsmith.*

Sarah Curran.

SARAH CURRAN 1782-1808

Oddly enough Sarah Curran did have a life before and after her indirect association with the Rising of 1803.

Hers was an unhappy home. At the age of eleven, the death of her sister Gertrude whom she loved, followed three years later by the separation of her parents, heightened her melancholic tendencies. From her earliest years she displayed a natural talent for music and was a proficient harpist.

Born in Rathfarnham, Dublin in 1782, her family's connection with the neighbouring Emmets led to her secret engagement to Robert. The killing of Lord Kilwarden during the rising led to her father's hostile reaction to the news of Sarah's secret liaison. For him the murder was an unforgiveable crime and caused him to disown his daughter and force her to leave home.

Alone, with Emmet's death leaving her a legacy of guilt, Sarah suffered a nervous breakdown or brain fever as it was then known. She went to Tivoli, Cork where the Penrose sisters helped restore her to partial health.

There she met and married a Captain Sturgeon who in 1805 was ordered to Sicily. Since Sarah had been diagnosed as consumptive the move was a welcome one. Three years later they were forced to leave because of political unrest. During the harrowing boat journey to England Sarah gave birth prematurely to a baby boy who died after they docked in Portsmouth. She herself died at Hythe, Kent 5 May 1808.

TERESA DEEVY
c. 1894-1963

Strange hats, mismatched clothes, Tessa cycled through the streets of Waterford in the fifties, completely deaf, yet managing somehow to avoid the bustling traffic. Some who saw her knew she had been a famous playwright, others did not. Today her work is forgotten.

Initially keen to be a teacher, she entered University College Dublin in 1913 and transferred to University College Cork when it was discovered that she had Menieres disease which left her deaf. On graduation, with her dreams dashed, she went to London to study lip-reading and returned to Ireland in 1919, determined to be a playwright.

Born in Kilkenny on 21 January 1894, her mother, Mary, encouraged her as a child to write stories about everyday events and was ambitious for her to become a novelist. Tessa's earliest efforts were published in the school magazine at the Ursuline Convent, but her talents lay in other directions too. She was second soprano in the school choir and received an honours certificate for piano playing. Besides this, for a year she played half-back in a hockey team that never lost a match! It was inevitable, in the light of her activities, that she should take a stance politically. She joined Cumann na mBan, despite her mother's disapproval.

Politics, religion (she was a devout Catholic) and land were the dominant themes in the plays she began to send to the Abbey at the age of twenty five. At last, one was accepted by Lennox Robinson, who later became an encouraging friend. Between 1930 and 1936 six of her plays were produced at the Abbey but *Temporal Powers* was the one which launched her as a fully-fledged dramatist and won an Abbey prize. *Katie Roche* was her most popular work and *Wild Goose* was the last to be staged there. In the late thirties the Abbey neglected her works and she mostly wrote radio plays for RTE and the BBC.

Tessa Deevy died in Maypark Nursing Home, Waterford in January 1963, never having heard her own plays being performed. The present neglect of her work is a great loss to Irish theatre.

KATE DEMPSEY
1893-1984

Not many women are elected to public office at the age of 74. Kate Dempsey was. Born on the Chord Road, Drogheda, County Louth in 1893, Kate lived there until 1925 when she married Vincent Dempsey and moved to Sandyford Terrace in the same town where she lived until her death nearly sixty years later.

A founder member of Cumann na mBan, Cumann na nGaedhl and the Irish Housewives Association, Kate was the first dispatch agitant of the 1st Eastern Division of the South Louth Brigade during the War of Independence and became the first woman in Drogheda to receive a military pension for her part in that struggle.

In 1960, she stood for local elections failing by only six votes to be elected. In 1967, she was elected to Drogheda Corporation becoming the first woman to be elected to that body since its establishment in 1412.

She retired from public life in 1974, having been a champion of the under-privileged. Kate died in October 1984 after a long and active career.

MÁIRÍN DE VALERA
1912-1984

Born in Dublin 13 June 1912, Máirín de Valera was a naturalist of the old school and invariably preferred to study her favourite plants in their natural environment, rather than under laboratory conditions. In 1947 she was appointed to the Lectureship in Botany and later to the Professor-ship in University College Galway.

Her life-long interest lay in the study of seaweeds and her early research in this field was carried out in Sweden at the University of Lund. Her work in Ireland was devoted to an investiga-tion of the native seaweed flora, of which she possessed an unrivalled knowledge. She concentrated on the study of the red seaweeds and in her publications added numerous species to the flora of the west coast. Her wide

Máirín de Valera.

ranging interest in the subject is demonstrated by her *Topographical Guide to the Seaweed of Galway Bay*, which, although published in 1958, is still in demand today.

She died 7 August 1984.

MARGARET SARAH DOCKRELL 1850-1926

Margaret Sarah Dockrell was educated at Alexandra College where she won a scholarship. In 1898, when the Local Government Act allowing women to be elected to district councils was passed, she contested a seat on the Urban District Council of Blackrock and was elected councillor. She was subsequently chosen deputy Vice Chairman *(sic)* and afterwards obtained the position of Vice Chairman *(sic)*. In

Margaret Sarah Dockrell.

1906, she became the first Chairwoman of an Urban Council.

She belonged to the Irish Women's Suffrage and Local Government Association and represented the association in a deputation which waited upon the British Prime Minister, Sir Henry Campbell Bannerman, on 19 May 1906 to urge the extension of women's suffrage to parliamentary elections.

She remained one of the ablest and most active women to take part in public affairs in Ireland up until her death in 1926 at the age of 76.

ELLEN DUNCAN 1850-1937

Ellen Duncan was a talented pianist, a successful journalist, an energetic organiser and she was single-minded in her promotion of modern art and living artists. Although it is a popular legend that the United Arts Club was founded by WB Yeats or by AE (George Russell), she herself founded the United Arts Club in 1907 and was the catalyst which enabled the most distinguished artists of the time to meet on neutral ground.

Hugh Lane, art connoisseur, collector, dealer, and patriot appointed her first Curator of the Municipal Gallery of Modern Art when it opened in Harcourt Street in January, 1908.

She reluctantly left Ireland for France in 1922 with her civil servant husband when he retired from his post in the Teachers' Pensions Office. After an unsettled few years she parted from him on ideological grounds and returned to Dublin hoping to resume her former activities in the Arts Club of the new Ireland. She is rarely remembered as the first Curator of the city's Municipal Gallery of Modern Art. Ellen Duncan was an active and tireless patron of the arts, and one who deserves Dublin's gratitude and admiration.

ELIZABETH FARREN
Countess of Derby
c. 1759-1829

As a child Elizabeth Farren used to beat the drums as the strolling company of players made their entrance into a provincial town. While still young she showed such promise on the stage that she quickly became a public favourite. Born in Cork, her father's drinking habits bankrupted the family and caused his early death. Consequently, her mother resumed a career as an actress in England and it was she who introduced Elizabeth to the stage.

Elizabeth's tall slender frame made her unsuitable for male parts and, after one disastrous attempt, she wisely left them to her rival and compatriot, Peg Woffington, who excelled in them. She made her first appearance in London in 1777 as Kate Hardcastle in *She Stoops to Conquer* by Oliver Goldsmith. Her reception was by no means enthusiastic but at Drury Lane the following year the audience was more than appreciative. She played in the works of Elizabeth Inchbald, one of Ireland's first women dramatists, appearing as Mrs Euston in her play *I'll*

Tell You What in August 1785.

Her success and gentle temperament gained her access to the fashionable world where she met the Earl of Derby. It is interesting to note that his first wife, Lady Betty Hamilton, was the only daughter of Elizabeth Gunning. The Earl courted Elizabeth for several years without any luck. However, when Lady Hamilton died, she accepted his proposal of marriage. In April 1797 Elizabeth took her leave of the stage in her favourite character of Mrs Teazle in *School for Scandal*. On 8 May 1797 she married the Earl.

Elizabeth Farren from the painting by Sir Thomas Lawrence.

ELIZABETH FLANAGAN
c. 1880-1962

Elizabeth Flanagan was the first woman mayor of Sligo. She held strong nationalist views throughout her life and in her earlier years was a founder member of Sligo Cumann na mBan.

Throughout the troubles and up until the split after the Treaty signed in 1922 she sided with the irregulars on the Republican side. During the Civil War, the Flanagan home was often a refuge for irregulars on the run. Eamon de Valera and Frank Aiken were among the notable visitors.

In 1923, when her husband was sentenced to six months imprisonment, she looked after the family grocery and provision business in High Street, Sligo. A member of Sligo Corporation and deeply humanitarian in her outlook, she fought for alterations in the lunch hour for children so that mothers could avoid the preparation of two meals. She died in June, 1962.

ELIZABETH GURLEY FLYNN
1890-1964

A confidante of James Connolly on his visit to the USA and a woman who helped raise bail for Jim Larkin when he was imprisoned there, Elizabeth Gurley Flynn, the 'Rebel Girl' of Joe Hill's famous song, led a rich and colourful life. Her activities varied from travelling with Mother Jones throughout America organising miners and textile workers into the 'Wobbley' movement to campaigning with Margaret Sanger for birth control freedom.

At sixteen years of age she already demonstrated her ability as a public speaker and as a street orator for the growing trade union movement and in 1912 became notorious for her involvement with the Lawrence Textile Workers Strike in Massachussets.

Much taken with the cause of labour prisoners she became a leading speaker in the International Campaign for the release of the martyrs Sacco and Vanzetti. In 1961 she was elected chairwoman of the American Communist Party. Imprisoned many times during her outstanding career, she died in 1964.

Elizabeth Gurley Flynn.

Elizabeth Flanagan, Sligo's first woman Mayor.

M. E. FRANCIS
1859-1930

Born of an Anglo-Irish family at Killiney Park, near Dublin, Mary grew up in Queen's County (present day County Laois). As a child Mary and her sisters (two of whom became writers) wrote fiction and founded their own family magazines. Mary's own first published short story appeared in *The Irish Monthly* and throughout her long career she wrote many religiously influenced stories.

Her *Daughters of the Soil* (1895) was the first novel to be published serially in the weekly edition of *The Times*. Besides many novels and short stories, Mary also wrote her reminiscences, *The Things of a Child*.

Her fiction takes up themes which are distinctly, resoundingly feminist and, if melodrama intrudes, Mary's ability to appeal to her readers' emotions explains her great popularity during her writing career. Several of her novels, particularly *The Story of Mary Dunne* (1913) and *Miss Erin* (1898) are serious examinations of the evils of Irish society, especially as they affect the lives of women.

She died in 1930. Her work has been neglected in recent years.

BEEZIE GALLAGHER
c. 1860-1951

Following the Great Blizzard of 1947,Beezie Gallagher was rescued from Cottage Island in Lough Gill in

Sligo suffering from malnutrition. Although in her early eighties, confinement of any sort, in particular that of the County Home, was unbearable to her and she returned after one week of recuperation to her home.

Born in the 1860s and orphaned at sixteen, Beezie, a nickname for Bridget, was reared on Cottage Island in Lough Gill. Her early years were spent as housemaid to the Wynne family.

She later went back to the Island she loved and in her solitude turned to nature for companionship. Stories of swans sitting in her kitchen and eating from her hand, or of a visitor banned from her island for throwing stones at a friendly rat, reflect the gentleness and warmth of her character.

At Beezie's there was always a welcome kettle on the boil. W B Yeats was a frequent visitor to this famed 'wise woman' and teller of tales. He came to recite verse and relate the affairs of the outside world. Beezie died on the island she loved in 1951. She had visited Sligo town on Christmas Eve and had rowed out to her home from Dooney Rock nearby. Friends watched her until she finally landed. When they rowed over some days later to cut timber for her, they found her burned to death in her island home.

Beezie is still remembered in Sligo and Cottage Island is now known as Beezie's Island.

Beezie Gallagher on Cottage Island, Lough Gill.

The Gunning Sisters.

EILEEN GRAY
1879-1976

Eileen Gray, designer and architect, loved flying and in the early twenties she flew on the first airmail service in America from New Mexico to Acupulco. She also accompanied Latham on an unsuccessful channel crossing in 1909 and during the First World War was an ambulance driver.

Eileen was born in Enniscorthy, County Wexford and having completed a private education, studied painting at the Slade School in London. She was apprenticed to Sugawara, a Japanese lacquer craftsman. In 1907 she moved to Paris and took an apartment in Rue Bonaparte in which she lived until her death. About 1919 she opened a gallery in 217 Fauborg St Honoré, selling rugs and furniture which she made and designed.

In 1925 she turned to architecture and began to build two houses at Roquebrune. A special issue of *Architecture Vivante* featured one which had murals by Le Corbusier, a close friend of hers. The other became the home of Graham Sutherland, the artist. *Wendinegn* a leading Dutch review, devoted an entire issue to her work in 1924. In April 1975 she was made honorary fellow of the Royal Institute of Architects in Ireland. She died in Paris on 31 October 1976.

THE GUNNING SISTERS
MARIA 1733-1760
ELIZABETH
1734-1790

George Anne Bellamy came upon the distressed Gunning sisters in Great Britain Street near Dominick Street, then the centre of fashionable living in Dublin. The mother of the famous Gunning 'beauties' was ambitious for their launch into society and had moved to Dublin from Castle Coote, Roscommon to realise her dreams. But accumulated debt brought them to the sorry state of poverty in which George Anne Bellamy found them. She proved a great friend giving them money and introducing them to Peg Woffington and David Garrick. Peg lent them dresses from her theatrical wardrobe for a ball at Dublin Castle. The sisters Maria and Elizabeth were a sensation and the Viceroy advised the mother to take them to England as soon as possible.

In April 1751 at the ages of seventeen

and eighteen they were presented to London society and were an instant success. Crowds mobbed them in order to get a look at the 'beauties'. Elizabeth was proposed to on the night of 13 February 1752 and married at midnight to the Duke of Hamilton with the ring of a bed curtain as no other was available at that hour. A fortnight later Maria married the Earl of Coventry. In 1760 Lady Coventry died, perhaps from overuse of cosmetics which contained lead but more likely from consumption. She left behind her a son and two daughters. Ten thousand people flocked to see her coffin.

Elizabeth, meanwhile, was widowed in 1759 and later married John Campbell the future Duke of Argyll. Twice a duchess, she was appointed Lady of the Bedchamber to the Queen and was made a peeress in her own right. She died at the age of fifty six.

FRANCOISE HENRY 1902-1982

On a cycling tour of Ireland in 1926 Francoise Henry, graduate of the Sorbonne and of the Ecole du Louvre, was captivated by the richness and variety of the early Christian sculpture to be found in this country. On her return to Paris she discussed the material she had collected with Focillon, her teacher, and he immediately recognised its outstanding qualities. Irish sculpture became the principal subjet for her degree of 'docteur d'état', and Ireland was to become her second home. During her years of study she developed her gift of

drawing and both in her thesis and in all her subsequent publications the line illustrations were all her own.

In 1932 she gained her doctorate and an appointment in the French Department of UCD. This enabled her to continue her research into Irish art and to take part in numerous excavations her favourite being Skellig Michael. Her first book was in English *Irish Art in the Early Christian Period.* Published in 1940 it became a text book for all students of the subject.

In 1934 she inaugurated the Purser-Griffiths series of lectures on the history of painting, the only course of its kind in Ireland. In retrospect it is clear that this course was instrumental in developing the great interest in art which has so recently occurred in Ireland.

Francoise was essentially a country-woman with a practical knowledge and love of the countryside. Her deeply Christian outlook gave her perhaps the depth of understanding of the early Christian tradition in Ireland so evident in her writing. She died in her native Auxerre, France on 10 February 1982.

HILARY HERON 1923-1977

Always an artist who combined a sense of humour with a true flair for exploring unusual arrangements of technique and materials, Hilary Heron, the Dublin sculptor, spent most of her childhood in New Ross, County Wexford and Coleraine in

County Derry. She went to the National College of Art and Design in Dublin where she won three of the Taylor prizes in succession. In 1947 she was awarded the first Mainie Jellett Memorial Travelling Scholarship for her work in carved wood, limestone and marble. She went to Italy and France in the same year to study Romanesque carvings.

She helped to found the Irish Exhibition of Living Art in Dublin and first exhibited there in 1943. She also represented Ireland with Louis Le Brocquy at the Venice Biennale in 1956.

In 1950 and 1953 she held her own one woman shows at the Victor Waddington Galleries, Dublin. It was during the 1950s that she began to work in metal, achieving a greater delicacy of effect. She travelled in Asia, America and Europe and her works are in private and public collections in many countries. She died aged 54 on 28 April 1977.

ST ITA (otherwise ITE or MITA, died *c.*AD570)

Ita, best known as a saint was born near Drum, County Waterford and is said to have been of royal descent and to have first been named Deirdre. A contemplative, she founded a school and convent at Killedy (Cill Ide) near Newcastle, West County Limerick.

Ita was St Brendan's spiritual director and his adventurous spirit can be attributed to his attendance at her school.

Ita's record on women's rights cannot be faulted. When one of the nuns in her convent became pregnant and the local bishop insisted on her expulsion, Ita stood by the woman. She was allowed to stay in the convent and when the child, a girl, was born, Ita brought her up as her own.

St Ita died in Killedy about 570. Many educational establishments have been named after her.

ROSAMUND JACOB 1888-1960

Rosamund Jacob was born in Waterford in 1888, the child of a Quaker family. She absorbed and adopted all their beliefs and opinions — which differed in almost every respect from those of her class and contemporaries, most notably in relation to Irish independence, religious freedom, women's rights and animal rights.

She lived in Dublin from 1920 until her death in 1960, and became an accomplished author and a courageous person in spite of the reticence and lack of self-confidence which resulted from her isolated childhood. An ardent suffragette and a member of Sinn Fein, her intense love of Ireland, its countryside, mythology, and culture informs everything she wrote. Four of her published books are *Callaghan* (1920), *The Troubled House* (1938), *The Rebel's Wife* (1957), *The Raven's Glenn* (1960). But her major achievement and most outstanding work was on *The Rise of the United Irishmen* (1937) of which Stephen Gwynn wrote: 'It is a work of real

Rosamund Jacob.

importance. No student of the period, which is crucial for all modern history, can neglect it.' She continued to write throughout her life and worked on committees, (as a secretary) and in various clubs, organisations and societies. Her passionately held beliefs and high ideals gave her many loyal, admiring and affectionate friends.

Dorothy Jordan from the portrait by George Romney.

DOROTHY JORDAN 1762-1816

In 1777 Dorothy Jordan was assistant to a milliner at Dame Street, Dublin. In 1779 she made her first recorded appearance on the stage at Crow Street Theatre, Dublin, later playing in Cork and her native Waterford. She played under the name of Miss Francis so as not to upset her parents.

However the harrassment of her manager obliged her to leave for London accompanied by her mother and sister. Taking the name of Mrs Jordan she joined a company playing the Yorkshire circuit.

In 1785 she went to Drury Lane, London, winning a name for herself in comedy, in particular 'breeches parts' and tomboy roles. In 1790 she became the acknowledged mistress or common law wife of the Duke of Clarence (later William IV) and for twenty years they lived happily together with their nine children. About 1811 a separation occurred and an annuity of £4,400 was agreed upon. But in August 1815 Dorothy fled to France from her many creditors and awaited settlement of her affairs. She died some months later at St Cloud on 3 July 1816.

BRIDGET KENNY *c.* 1860-1930

Bridget Kenny, one of the earliest musicians to record on phonograph cylinders, was known as the 'Queen of the Fiddlers'. She earned her keep and managed to support a family of thirteen by playing for a pittance along the highways and byways of Dublin. How many of those who heard her realised that she outclassed all competitors as a traditional violinist at the annual Feiseanna, winning first prize with almost monotonous regularity? She first started to play the fiddle when seven years old. 'I'm entirely self taught and proud of it,' she claimed. Her natural talent should have been regarded as a national asset, but no. Despite the tumultuous applause of the concert halls, she was permitted to return to the streets of the Irish capital and play for coins from purses often emptier than her own. Only in Ireland would a musician of such talent and ability remain un-appreciated and unnoticed. Bridget's talent was an outstanding contribution to the world of Irish music.

Bridget Kenny.

Drede, the Bishop of Ossory, who stood to gain the Kyteler fortune should she be found guilty. His greed obliged him to convict her of many outrageous crimes, including fornication with Robert Artisson, a spirit with whom it is quoted she had a 'strange and unholy association'.

Alice escaped arrest, principally because her nephew was the Chancellor of Ireland and the bishop could not obtain a warrant. Her supporters avenged themselves by incarcerating the bishop, after which Alice coolly indicted him for defamation of character.

She fled to England, abandoning her maid, Petronilla de Meath, who was the first woman in Ireland to be burned as a witch and who died claiming her mistress, Alice Kyteler, was the most powerful sorceress in the world.

ALICE KETTLE/KYTELER – 14th Century

The fourth husband of Alice Kyteler of Kilkenny became the victim of a strange wasting disease, similar, so it was said, to that of his three predecessors. The finger of suspicion was inevitably pointed at Alice, whose private bedroom was forcibly entered in the search for evidence. There were discovered several items indisputably connected with witchcraft — a sacramental wafer with a print of the devil and a pipe of mysterious ointment.

Her prosecution was taken on by a fanatical witch-hunter, Richard Le

Alice Kettle's house, Kilkenny.

LUCY OLIVE KINGSTON
1892-1969

Lucy Olive Kingston (nee Lawrenson) was born in County Wicklow in 1892 but lived all her life in Dublin, where she died in 1969. She was actively interested in the suffragette movement, in peace and international affairs. She belonged to the Women's Social and Progressive League and to the Irish Housewife's Association, which had an international sub-committee affiliated to the Women's International League for Peace and Freedom.

In the early 1930s she became a Quaker and worked with Quakers and others in helping refugees from Germany before and during the Second World War, giving hospitality to many in her home in Dalkey.

In 1949 she attended a peace conference in India, and served on many peace committees for the next twenty years. Her last committee work was the arranging of a commemorative plaque for Helen Chenevix to be affixed to the Louie Bennett Memorial Seat in St. Stephen's Green.

Lucy Olive Kingston.

EMILY LEDWITH
1893-1983

Emily Elliot came to Dublin in 1914 from Glasson, Westmeath. Soon after she was apprenticed to Hughes Brothers Confectionery in Ranelagh which when completed gave her employment in many well known establishments at the turn of the century among them The Bonne Bouche, Cafe Cairo and Robert Roberts of Grafton Street.

But for Emily, this was not enough. Coming from a revolutionary family she naturally gravitated to the Pearses and MacDonaghs of her day. She became a founder member of Cumann na mBan and at the start of the 1916 Rising it was she who undertook to mobilise her colleagues into battle.

She was assigned to the Four Courts garrison as a first aid nurse and Father Augustine's testimonial testifies to her work in this area. She and her husband opened a small hotel in Dorset Street, Dublin, where her training was again put to use. The house was raided regularly by the Black and Tans who knew the

Ledwiths sheltered men on the run. In her later years she took an active part in politics. When she was in her eighties she became a patient in Sally Park Nursing Home, Firhouse, County Dublin where she died 3 March 1983.

LADY DOROTHY LOWRY-CORRY 1885-1967

Born in County Fermanagh, Dorothy Lowry-Corry was one of thirteen children of the fourth Earl of Belmore. Their home at Castlecoole County

While refusing ever to have her photograph taken, Dorothy Lowry Corry used the camera extensively in her work. She recorded her discovery of the 'Bishop's' stone above at Killadeas Graveyard, Co. Fermanagh.

Fermanagh contained a comprehensive library and collection of documents. Dorothy made good use of it when developing her interest in local history and genealogy which later extended into archaeology particularly of the early Christian period.

Her oldest archaeological association was with the Royal Society of Antiquaries of which she became vice-president. Among the papers she contributed to the proceedings of the Royal Irish Academy, perhaps the most important was the recording of the Boa Island and Lustymore stone figures.

She became the representative for County Fermanagh when the Ancient Monuments Advisory Committee was established by the Ministry of Finance. In 1934 the Committee decided to undertake a survey of the monuments of all periods in the north of Ireland. Dorothy took on the work of surveying County Fermanagh becoming an indefatigable field worker. Among her discoveries was the megalithic tomb at Corracloona County Leitrim. She contributed many articles to the *Ulster Journal of Archaeology* from its first issue in 1938. She died on 22 March 1967.

DOLORES LYNCH 1948-1982

Dolores Lynch was born in Dublin in 1948. She was a prostitute who fought courageously against harrassment from the Guards and violence by the pimps. She bravely testified against pimps in the Court resulting in much physical abuse over many years. She herself succeeded after several attempts in retiring from the 'game' and became a ward worker in St James' Hospital, Dublin where she was dedicated to the old people in her care. During her holidays she tended to invalids in Lourdes and the highlight of her later years was a private audience with the Pope.

She was murdered in January 1982 by a pimp who bore her a grudge for testifying against him in court.

MARY ANN McCRACKEN
c. 1770-1866

The McCracken family in Rosemary Lane, Belfast, strongly opposed the arrival of Henry Joy's "illegitimate" daughter, Maria. But they had Mary Ann, his sister, to confront and with characteristic spirit, she overrode their prejudice and brought her niece up in the household.

Mary Ann McCracken was swept into activism in the movement of 1798 against British control of Ireland. Born in Belfast, she went to one of the first co-educational schools of that period and this perhaps accounts for her passionate commitment to social reform. Mary Ann withdrew from radical politics after the execution of her friend Thomas Russell in 1803 and ran a muslin business with her sister Margaret until its closure in 1815.

Influenced by the English prison reformer, Elizabeth Fry, she joined with middle class women to form a Ladies' Committee to devote their

Mary Ann McCracken and her niece Maria. (Miniature, owned by H. A. Aitchison, taken from Mary Ann McCracken *by Mary McNeil.* [Alan Figgis, 1960]

attention to Belfast's Workhouse. She argued and gained improvements for poorhouse women in clothing and education. She developed the idea of an infants' school, which actually got off the ground for a while. She opposed slavery and was one of the committee set up in Belfast to abolish the use of climbing boys as chimney sweep helpers. She campaigned tirelessly for better conditions for children working in factories. Mary Ann died in Belfast in 1866.

ESTHER Mac GREGOR
1893-1980

On International Women's Day 1976, Esther McGregor was given a standing ovation in Dublin's Mansion House.

The platform, which included women from Chile, South Africa and the Soviet Union and the large audience, were acknowledging the fact that Esther and a small group of women activists had been celebrating Women's Day in gatherings in their own homes in the early part of the century. Esther was a symbol of the continuity of the struggle for women's rights.

Born in 1893 she first became involved in politics through attendance at the Connolly Workers' Education Club which in the period of 1928-29 organised weekly lectures and classes in Marxist economics. It was no mere debating society as it assisted also in organising unemployed demonstrations, a socialist children's organisation and in protest activities against the frame-up of Sacco and Vanzette, the Negro Patterson Boys, Tom Mooney and J B

Esther MacGregor.

McNamara who was then the longest incarcerated prisoner in the world.

When the Irish Revolutionary Workers' Groups (RWG) were formed in April 1930, one of their first achievements was the launching of the paper 'The Irish Workers' Voice', the first issue of which appeared on May Day. By the third issue Esther McGregor was running a women's column as well as contributing separate articles on women's social and economic questions.

She worked with the 'Irish Friends of Republican Spain' during the Spanish Civil War. It was a terrible blow to her when her son Liam was killed. The shock of his death was intensified by the circumstances. He fell in the last hours of the last battle of the 15th International Brigade in Spain.

She was a member of the Management Committee of the Ballyfermot and Inchicore Co-Operative Society. That 'Co-Op' was the target of a vicious attack by clerical and business interests combined which eventually succeeded in getting it closed down in the 1950s.

She died on the 4th November 1980.

NORAH McGUINNESS 1903-1981

In 1939, Dublin's department store, Brown Thomas, was the stylish owner of window designs and shop displays somewhat in the style of those in New York designed by Salvador Dali. The

Nora McGuinness.

artistic hand beind these striking arrangements belonged to Derry born Norah McGuinness who learned the technique in America when she went there in 1937 for exhibition.

Mainly a landscape painter, concentrating on water colour and gouache, she switched in the 1940s to paint predominantly in oils. Earlier in her career, having studied in art schools in Dublin and London, she went to Paris in 1929 on the advice of Mainie Jellett and worked there under André Lohte. During this time she illustrated many books, including Sterne's *A Sentimental Journey* — which was her first commission, and several others by Elizabeth Bowen, Yeats, Maria Edgeworth and Elizabeth Hamilton.

In 1940 she had her first exhibition with the Royal Hibernian Academy of which she became an honorary member in 1957. A founder member of the Irish Exhibition of Living Art, she became president for a period of five years in 1944 on the death of Mainie Jellett. She exhibited with Nano Reid at the Venice Biennale in 1950. A fine artist and one of whom we can be proud, Norah McGuinness died in 1981.

SUSAN LANGSTAFF MITCHELL 1866-1926

Susan Langstaff Mitchell was a prominent member of the Arts Club, Dublin many of whose patrons were featured in her light satiric verse. Born in Carrick-on-Shannon, County Leitrim, she was sent to Dublin at six

years of age, after her father's death, to live with two aunts. She attended a private school in Morehampton Road Dublin and also had lessons in music dancing and drawing. In 1900 an illness which impaired her hearing sent her to London where she stayed with the family of John B Yeats.

In 1901 she became editor of *The Irish Homestead* later edited by George Russell in 1905. She worked with him against in 1926 as sub-editor of the *Irish Statesman* to which she also contributed stories and articles. Her first collection of verse *Aids to the Immortality of Certain Persons - Charitably Administered* appeared in 1908. In it she satirised a number of notable people in public life and literature. In 1916 she contributed a study of George Moore to a series entitled Irishmen Today. She died 1926.

ELLEN MULLINS *c.* 1880-1956

Women came from miles around to ask Ellen Fitzgerald to deliver their children and it is said that she rarely lost a child or a mother. She was a familiar and welcome sight, cycling the roads of Kilkishan, Co. Clare in 1915 and later, after her marriage to John Mullins, she progressed to the pony and trap. This safe and lucky midwife charged her fees in accordance with people's circumstances; farming families perhaps ten shillings and labouring families a couple of chickens or maybe half-a-crown.

The youngest of eleven children, her mother died in childbirth and the family moved from Castleconnel to Killbarron, County Clare. It is believed that Ellen was related to Biddy Early, the wise woman of Kilbarron. Nurse Mullins trained in the Coombe Hospital in Dublin in 1912 and having completed her midwifery course, she stayed on there for another three years or so. She went to the Scarriff Union and arrived in Kilkishan around 1915. She was paid twenty five pounds a year at that time and she had to pay five shillings a week for her room and lodgings.

In the 1930s she became the Registrar of Births, Marriages and Deaths for the area and continued this work into the fifties. She remained a midwife up to about 1942 when she was in her seventies and in the last years her foster daughter, also a midwife, assisted her. Nurse Mullins is fondly remembered by many who knew and appreciated her skill, dedication and gentleness.

Woodcut by Harry Kernoff (RHA) of the 'Turf Girl' for which Delia Murphy was the model.

DELIA MURPHY
1902-1971

'Delia Murphy come here. Let you take Tom by the hand and bring him to school.' Thus began the career of Ireland's 'Ballad Queen', Delia Murphy of Roundfort Mayo. Tom Maughan, the traveller's son, knew the ballads of the countryside and Delia learned them all on her way to and from school. From him she learned *If I were a Blackbird* and made it famous all over Ireland.

The next stage in her education was the Dominican Convent, Eccles Street, Dublin where she sang in the choir until she was put out. Here she met her life-long friend, Margaret Burke Sheridan.

In University College, Galway, she graduated with a B Comm. She discovered during these years her talent for 'tinkering' or composing from bits and pieces of old ballads, and sang at many student concerts.

Her recording career began in the 1930s and in an extraordinary way. John McCormack was practising in the studio and Delia corrected his phrasing. A representative from HMV recording company was listening and was so impressed by her voice he asked to make a record of Irish ballads. She did, nearly a hundred songs and was top of the top twenty in Ireland.

As her fame grew she became one of

the most requested singers on Radio Eireann and even the BBC referred to her as 'Our Delia'. Film offers came and she appeared in 'The Island Man', filmed in the Blaskets. She was invited to America to pursue this career but the care of a young family prevented her from doing so. Delia was an extrovert, who liked and was liked by many people. She detested meanness and of one character she said, 'he wouldn't give you the itch for fear you'd have the comfort of scratching it.' She loved Ireland and sang for the ordinary folk who came to her concerts. 'I sing for the real people of the gods,' she said.

ÉIBHLÍN DHUBH NÍ CHONAILL
c. 1743-1800

At fifteen Éibhlín Dhubh Ní Chonaill of Derrynane, Kerry, one of a family of twenty two, was married off to the elderly O'Connor of Iveragh. As he lay dying six months later, tradition has it that she was cracking nuts for herself, unperturbed.

In 1767, she met and was instantly attracted to Art O Laoghaire, the flamboyant captain of the Hungarian Hussars who had just returned from serving the Empress Maria Theresa. Noted for his boldness and fiery temperament, her family rejected him as suitor. Nevertheless she married him against their express wishes c. 19 December 1767.

They lived in magnificent style in Macroom, Cork until 4 May 1773. On this day the father of her two children was killed by the High Sherriff's bodyguard in Carrignimia, Cork. Éibhlín's lament or caoineadh over Art's dead body is one of the greatest in the Irish language, and is also one of its greatest love poems. Containing many elements of the traditional caoineadh, it is preserved in many versions and fragments in Irish oral tradition.

Neilí Ní Dhómhaill.

NEILÍ NÍ DHÓMHNAILL 1907-1984

Poor eyesight in early childhood forced Neilí Ní Dhómhnaill to sit in the company of older people, while her family and friends went out in the evenings, dancing or visiting. This was how she acquired her vast wealth of traditional story and song.

Born in Ranafast, County Donegal in 1907, she traced her ancestry to the O'Donnell poets of Donegal. An inspired and inspiring singer, and a wonderful storyteller, she combined these two art forms into one. For her, the story which preceded any song, Irish or English, was equally important as the song itself.

As is often the case, the diminishing power of one faculty seemed to heighten another and Neilí had only to hear a song once to know it. The pain accompanying deteriorating eyesight increased over the years and even when she was completely blind, it continued. This did not mean that she retired from life. She remained active, keeping house, cleaning, cooking and was proud of a home where everything had its place. She took up knitting, using the most intricate stitches, and worked as a home knitter, producing a minimum of two Aran sweaters each week. And how did she measure them? Her sense of touch was such that she had only to feel the width of a person's shoulders to know their size.

Towards the end of her life she composed songs, encouraged by a Radio na Gaeltachta competition for new words to old airs. For two consecutive years she won first prize. Neilí's songs and her spirit live on through the singing of her nieces Tríona and Máiréad Ní Dhómhnaill. A deeply religious woman, she believed strongly in the power of prayer and had many tales to tell of how hers had been answered.

SORCHA NÍ GHUAIRIM c. 1912-1976

At the age of fifteen Sorcha Ní Ghuairim moved from Carna, Galway to Dublin where her sister, Máire, helped her to find work teaching Irish for Conradh na Gaeilge. But her life was to include other areas as diverse as singing and journalism, singing being the one in which she was to make a name for herself. She obtained a Gaeltacht scholarship and studied commerce at UCG. Later she wrote for the periodicals *An tÉireannach* and *Ar Aghaidh* and taught Irish at Trinity College, Dublin. She became well known as an adjudicator of singing at Oireachtas na Gaeilge and recorded for Folkways Records in 1945. Her fine sean nós singing style was a first introduction for many people to this ancient and distinctive art.

In her twenties her health broke down and she went to live in England, making several trips to the United States to make recordings there. She died in London but was brought back to Carna and buried in Maighinis.

MÁIRE BHUÍ NÍ LAOGHAIRE 1774-1849

A renowned Cork poet, much folklore surrounds Máire Bhuí Ní Laoghaire in which she is described as a tall, imposing yellow haired woman who travelled the roads of Ireland with a blackthorn stick and a ready tongue and pen.

Her poetry included many patriotic verses and commemorates local battles and events. She was also one of the last poets to write 'aisling' or vision poetry.

The Irish saying 'Tá sé ráite riamh ná téann an fhilíocht thar mhnaoi' — It is said that the gift of poetry cannot continue beyond a woman or ends with a woman, specifically related to Máire Bhuí and it is generally believed that she was the last of the great O'Laoghaire poets.

Catherine O'Brien in her studio.

CATHERINE (Kitty) O'BRIEN c. 1881-1963

On wet days in Dublin, Kitty O'Brien was a familiar and much loved figure in the Fitzwilliam area, cycling steadily along, holding an umbrella over her head.

Originally from County Clare, she went to work at the Tower of Glass stained glass studio, Dublin, in 1904, having studied in the Metropolitan School of Art, where she was influenced by A E Childe. She remained with the studio, closely associated with the revived tradition of stained glass in this country until its demise, and hers, in 1963.

She was a devout Christian and worshipped in Christ Church Cathedral for forty years. At the great festivals she was in charge of the floral arrangements and decorations of the Cathedral Sanctuary and as a lover of flowers, had a tremendous eye for colours that blended and glowed.

During the years 1904 to 1963 she produced many designs and over a hundred richly coloured windows for churches at home and abroad. Perhaps her finest work is in the eastern window of the Church of Ireland church at Carrickmines. This presents a single theme from several scenes of Christ's life. Her Kinsale window is gemlike in the setting of a mediaeval building beside the famous harbour. The rich blue of the sea in the fishing scene recalls Galilee, its boats and nets. An order for a set of stations of the cross on circular panels for a church at Vero Beach in Florida, gave Kitty particular satisfaction.

A luminous and dignified window by Patrick Pollen was later erected to Catherine O'Brien's memory in the chapel of St Laurence O'Toole in Christ Church Cathedral.

GRACE O'MALLEY
c. 1530-1600

According to tradition, the source of most of her history, Grainne Mhaol, 'Grace of the cropped hair'', was a bold and independent leader. Described as 'a most famous feminine sea captain', she is reputed to have visited Queen Elizabeth I in London and spoken to her as one queen to another.

Born probably in County Mayo, she was of noted sea roving stock and spent her childhood on the islands off the western coast of Ireland. She married twice, first to an O'Flaherty and then in 1582 to Richard Burke, chief of his clann in Mayo. After his death in 1586, she was arrested by Sir Richard Bingham and accused of plundering the Aran Islands. A gallows was pre-pared for her execution. She was released on a pledge from her son-in-law, Richard Burke, and when he rebelled against the English, she fled to Ulster and sought sanctuary in the O'Neill stronghold. She was unable to return owing to the loss of her ships.

Grace O'Malley's Castle at Rockfleet, Co. Mayo.

Once again, she was pardoned by Queen Elizabeth and went back to Connaught, dying there in abject poverty a few years later. She is buried in Clare Island, Clew Bay, County Mayo.

ELIZA O'NEILL
c. 1791-1872

Eliza O'Neill was an actress of special interest. Her dramatic abilities were enough to make some members of her audience faint, and one poor creature was even made insane by seeing her performance of *Belvedere*, in Dublin. Hers was a phenomenal talent envied by contemporaries although it spanned no more than five years at its height.

Her father was stage manager of the Drogheda Theatre, and Eliza's first stage appearance was in her father's arms. At ten years of age she was playing the Duke of York to her father's hump-backed Richard the Third, and was spotted by a Mr Talbot from Belfast. He immediately offered her an engagement and the young Eliza insisted on the invitation extending to her entire family.

In October 1811, Crow Street Theatre, Dublin, boasted the presence of Eliza O'Neill, who stood in for another actress sacked for insisting on higher pay. It was the beginning of a superb career. John Kemble, over from England on contract, spied the young Eliza and persuaded her to try Covent Garden, once again she

Eliza O'Neill.

insisted that her family go along too. On 16 October 1814 at the age of twenty two Eliza made an enthralling debut as Juliet. She was a huge success. It is reported that Byron refused to see her act for fear of becoming an O'Neill convert, thereby defusing his enthusiasm for Edmund Kean, his favourite. 'I am resolved to continue un-O'Neilled,' he said.

Jane Austen records in one of her letters that 'she (Eliza) was an elegant creature'. In the summer of 1820 Eliza returned to Ireland and made her last appearance on 11 December. Seven days later she married William Wrixon Becher, then Member of Parliament for Mallow, who later became a baronet. Lady Becher led a quiet life in County Cork, rarely leaving home. One account tells of her going to the Garrick Club in London in later years to see her own portrait. Standing before it, she burst into tears, possibly remembering the fainting audiences, the frenzied applause and her own magnificent performances. Eliza lived to the great age of eighty one.

MOLLY O'REILLY
c. 1900-1950

Only fifteen years of age and already a member of the Irish Citizen Army, Molly O'Reilly trundled up Gardiner Street with a handcart full of guns from the Asgard and carefully placed them under her father's bed. Violently opposed to Sinn Fein, he never found out what lay beneath him, luckily for Molly.

Her politicisation began early when, as

Molly O'Reilly.

Hall on Palm Sunday, one week before the Rising occurred. The family opposed the proposition but Molly, true to form, left home in order to help.

On Easter Monday she marched to the GPO with the Citizen Army and was despatch carrier between it and the City Hall. When everything was over she went to Yorkshire to study nursing but, characteristically returned on hearing word of further unrest. She then joined Cumann na mBan and became 'digs' organiser for the I R A In her everyday work at the United Service Club St Stephen's Green she also proved invaluable. It is said that she once relieved six British soldiers of six pearl-handled pistols, removing them from the premises in a Jacobs' biscuit factory to O'Callaghans' Saddlery in Capel Street. In 1922 she remained Republican, was arrested on 1 March that year and was released 23 November after sixteen days hunger strike. One of Ireland's most active and dedicated freedom fighters, Molly O'Reilly died on 4 October 1950.

an eight year old, she attended Irish dancing classes at Liberty Hall. While she was there, the Big Strike of 1913 took place and she lent a hand in the soup kitchens, peeling potatoes and preparing vegetables. The speeches in Liberty Hall deeply impressed her, especially those of James Connolly. She was appalled at the living conditions of Dublin's poor and thus joined the Citizen Army and Clann na Gaedhl.

Her activities caught the attention of Connolly. He asked her would she be willing to take part in hoisting the Irish flag (green with a harp) over Liberty

SAIDIE PATTERSON
1906-1985

'If the men in the Movement passed more pubs and less resolutions we'd be a good deal better off.' So said Saidie Patterson, who at twelve years of age began working in the Belfast Linen Mills. She was active in her union, the Amalgamated Transport and General Workers' Union, and was prominent in many strikes to improve the conditions of the mainly female workforce.

Saidie Patterson.

Born of working class Methodist parents in 1906 on the Falls Road (where she remained all her life), Saidie was a woman dedicated to peace and was involved in a number of peace movements. After the Second World War she became involved with the Moral Rearmament Movement Group which promoted reconciliation between races and classes. Later she became a founder member of 'Women Together', which preceded the Peace People, in which she also developed an interest.

In 1978 she became the first person to be awarded the Methodist Peace Award for her efforts to bridge the divide between the two religious communities in northern Ireland. In all, she won five International Peace Awards and gave all the money to charities for children or arthritis sufferers, of which she was one.

In 1945 she played a leading role in the elections in which she saw her party, the Northern Ireland Labour Party, win several seats in the Belfast area. She died in January 1985.

NANO REID
1905-1981

The portraits painted by Drogheda's Nano Reid were bold and original with a raw honesty which disconcerted at least one of her sitters. He asked for his money back on seeing himself on canvas and Nano's career as a portrait painter ended. But this work was done out of economic necessity and she simply returned to landscape painting, unscathed by the experience.

An element of mystery prevails in the wild Irish countryside she depicted — scenes from County Donegal, Achill, County Mayo, Connemara, and her native Boyne Valley, County Meath are lively, direct and inventive. In later years she ceased using the Valley as a subject saying in an interview for radio in 1969: 'The place isn't the same since they started all the excavating. To me the mounds were interesting when you didn't know what was inside them.'

She had her first one-woman show in 1934 at the Gallery, St Stephen's Green which was considered to be premature. Her second was more successful in 1936 and moved to Drogheda in County Louth at the Mayor's request. During the 1930s she exhibited mainly with the Royal Hibernian Academy but from 1943 she switched to the Irish Exhibition of Living Art, the Dublin Painters and later the Independent Artists. In 1972 she won the Douglas Hyde gold medal. An artist of great merit, the works of Nano Reid are rightly included in many major collections, both in Ireland and Europe.

SHELAH RICHARDS 1903-1985

'Who is the girl with the head like a lion?' asked Yeats when he first saw Shelah Richards in the Arts Club, aged sixteen. She was later to play in his drama *The Player Queen*, a role glorified by Molly O'Neill and a daunting one for the young Richards,

since Yeats would allow no other actress to play the role for ten years after Molly O'Neill. At his request she also took over the Abbey School of Acting.

Shelah Richards was a major figure in Irish theatre and television for over fifty years and was one of the earliest producers when RTE television started. She produced many programmes besides drama, among them religious affairs and documentaries.

Born in 1903 and reared in Dublin, there was little in her family background to suggest a career on the stage. Indeed, it was said her father first heard of her acting when he was complimented on her success in the Abbey. But there was little to prevent this woman from forging a name for herself in the annals of theatrical history. Introduced to a new world by Lord Glenavy and Beatrice Elvery, the artist, she was soon acting in the Dublin Drama League and replaced Eileen Crow at twelve hours notice in the part of Mary Boyle in *Juno and the Paycock*. She created the role of Nora Clitheroe in the first production of *The Plough and the Stars* and became a friend of the author, Sean O'Casey. In 1938 she left the Abbey to got to New York with Gladys Cooper and A E Mathews to play in M J Farrell's (Molly Keane's) *Spring Meeting*. Despite advice to remain because of pending war, she returned to Dublin and her two children.

Her own company, which she ran so successfully during the war years in partnership with Michael Walsh, once witnessed audiences queueing as far as the Bank of Ireland in order to gain admittance. It is interesting to note

Shelah Richards.

that she was the producer of Siobhan MacKenna's first *Playboy*. Shelah Richards, a legend in her own lifetime, died after a short illness in Dublin in January 1985.

MÁIRE KEOHANE SHEEHAN
c. 1915-1975

A nurse and midwife by profession, Máire Keohane Sheehan was secretary of the Cork branch of the Irish Nurses' Organisation and was a consistent public agitator for the under-privileged.

She became a founder member of the Cork Socialist Party which nominated Michael O'Riordan as its candidate in the 1945 local election and the 1946 by-election. She was vice chairwoman of the Liam Mellowes branch of the Irish Labour Party in Cork, which was dissolved by the William Norton leadership in 1945.

A passionate and at times humorous speaker, she was well known in Labour and trade union circles in Cork City, West Cork and in Dublin. During her time in the Labour Party she was a member of its Administrative Council, being at all times a firm opponent of Labour's coalition with Fine Gael. She died in 1975 when she was chairwoman of the Cork Branch of the Communist Party of Ireland.

MARGARET BURKE SHERIDAN
1889-1958

When Terence MacSwiney died on hunger strike in Brixton Prison in 1920, the San Carlo Opera House in Naples was obliged to close because, it was announced: 'La Sheridan will not sing, her compatriot is dead.'

La Margherita Sheridan, as she was known in Italy, was born on the Mall in Castlebar and received her first music lessons in the Dominican Convent, Eccles Street, Dublin. It was here that she met and became firm friends with the 'Ballad Queen', Delia Murphy. A sponsored concert in the Theatre Royal provided her with the money to begin studying at the Royal College of Music in London. At this time she could not possibly have dreamt that one day her operatic successes would be commemorated in bronze in the La Scala opera house in Milan.

Guglielmo Marconi was so impressed by her singing that he made the necessary arrangements for her to continue her studies in Italy. Under the guidance of Martini and Emma Corelli, she blossomed into one of the greatest sopranos of all time, receiving a magnificent ovation at her operatic debut in La Constanzia, Rome. Toscanini heard her and invited her to sing Mimi in *La Bohème*. So outstanding was her performance here that it led to a further series of successful engagements in operas by Puccini. Pope Pius XI offered her the title Countess when he came into office, but characteristically she declined.

A severe illness in 1934 caused her to lose confidence in her ability as a performer and since she was a perfectionist and constantly sought excellence she retired and returned to Dublin. This great lady of the Italian Opera Houses died in St Vincent's Hospital, Dublin on 16 April 1958.

*Máire Keohane Sheehan in nurse's uniform
surrounded by family.*

FRANCES
SHERIDAN
c. 1724-1766

Frances Chamberlaine's father, a
clergyman, strongly disapproved of his
daughter's being taught to read and
write. So much so that her eldest
brother had to teach her in private.
Nevertheless, at fifteen she had written
a romance *Eugenia and Adelaide*, which
was published posthumously.

In 1745 she praised Thomas Sheridan,
manager of the Theatre Royal, Dublin,
both in verse and pamphlet, for
reprimanding a drunken patron. They
met and married in 1747.

On moving to London in 1754,
Samuel Richardson encouraged her to
write another novel. The result, *The*

Memoirs of Miss Biddulph, appeared in
1761 and was warmly received and
later translated into French and
German. She wrote several comedies,
The Discovery (1763) being the most
successful. To escape their creditors,
they moved to Blois, France where she
died 26 September 1766.

ENID MARY
STARKIE *c.* 1899-1970

Born in Killiney, County Dublin, Enid
Mary Starkie was educated at
Alexandra College and the Royal Irish
Academy of Music, Somerville
College, Oxford and the Sorbonne.

She worked as an assistant lecturer in
modern language at Exeter University

and then returned in 1929 to Somerville College as a lecturer. Her biographies of Baudelaire, Rimbaud and Flaubert brought her not only critical acclaim, but also an honorary doctorate from the Sorbonne, a prize from the French Academy, and she also had the distinction of being made a Chevalier of the Legion of Honour.

Her revealing account of life in Dublin and Oxford *A Lady's Child*, caused consternation among her family with its honesty. She died in Oxford in 1970.

MARGARET STOKES
c. 1820-1900

Margaret McNair Stokes grew up in a house in Dublin that was a centre of artistic and literary tastes. She was an excellent artist and was attracted by the beauty of the inscriptions on Irish stones.

She edited and added drawings of her own to an invaluable collection of Irish inscriptions belonging to Dr Petrie who died before they were published. They were entitled *Christian Inscriptions of the Irish Language* published in two quarto volumes. A further important work on Irish antiquities was *Notes on Irish Architecture* which was edited by Margaret Stokes and published in 1877 in two quarto volumes.

She also travelled in France and Italy in search of traces of Irish saints. Towards the close of her life she returned to the subject which had first engaged her attention, the High Crosses of Ireland.

Elected an Honorary member of the Irish Academy in 1876, she was unrivalled in her knowledge of Christian Ireland's former greatness. Margaret copied the originals of the intricate designs in the Book of Kells, made facsimile drawings of the Processional Cross of Cong, Ardagh Chalice, Shrine of Moedog and others. Her great work, descriptions and drawings of the sculptured Crosses of Ireland, was never finished, as she died on 20 September 1900.

MARY TIGHE
nee Blachford
c. 1772-1801

The beautiful surroundings of Wicklow and her own dreamy nature combined to inspire Mary Tighe to write *Psyche,* an allegory written and printed in 1805. It was received with a chorus of praise and Moore addressed a poem to her in honour of her achievement. However, when William Howitt came to Ireland in order to add her name to his book *The Homes and Haunts of Poets c.* 1900, he could uncover no information concerning Mary Tighe. Very little was known of her.

Born in Dublin in 1772, it is said, in true romantic spirit 'early death was pale upon her cheek' and she died at thirty eight, after many years of suffering with consumption. Her marriage in 1793 to her cousin, Henry Tighe of Rosanna, County Wicklow, proved unhappy. Mary appears to have been an ethereal character, completely unsuited to the harsh realities of everyday living. Soon after the marriage they went to London, where Henry, who was a barrister of the Middle Temple, mixed a good deal in society. By 1805, ill health obliged Mary to travel around seeking cures, all to no avail. On 24 March 1810 she died at Woodstock, County Wicklow. She is buried in her churchyard of Inistioge, where a monument has been erected to her memory.

Ironically, after her death, editions of her poem came out rapidly, two in 1811, and a long article in *The Quarterly Review* of May 1811 gave it high praise. A fifth edition came out in 1816 and it was printed in Philadelphia in 1813. Surprisingly, it was reprinted in 1853, proving that the verse which lightened Mary's solitude found a delighted audience and was not forgotten.

Mary Tighe.

KATHLEEN TIMONEY
c. 1889-1972

Kathleen Timoney, born in Killala, County Clare on 28 March 1889, was one of the first catholic women students to attend medical school in Galway. However, for some strange reason, her ambitions were considered suspect and she was called before the Bishop of Galway and threatened with excommunication should she continue. Undaunted and displaying exceptional courage for her time, she transferred to the Medical School, Cecilia Street, National University of Ireland, completed her studies and qualified as a doctor. For six months she worked in Temple Street Hospital, Dublin and was one of the earliest workers on behalf of St Ultan's Hospital for Children, also in Dublin.

Kathleen was active in the Easter Rising and was in contact with IRA headquarters. Although expecting her second child, she made some of the preliminary arrangements for the signalling of the *Aud* in Tralee Bay. On 3 May 1916, she gave birth to a boy whom she christened Pearse after the national hero of the day.

During the War of Independence, she was ordered by the IRA to stop all nationalist activities, including that of medical lecturer to Cumann na mBan, so as not to draw attention to her husband. He was a brigade medical officer and Kathleen and he had a secret attic in their house where seriously wounded members of the Active Service Units were treated until they could walk. Having a deep concern for victims of tuberculosis, she worked tirelessly in this area, along with her partner, who was County Tuberculosis Officer. She subsequently received a military service medal for her work during the War of

Independence. Kathleen Timoney died, aged eighty three at Mount Carmel Hospital, Churchtown, having lived in Dublin from 1938.

ÉIBHLÍN BEAN UÍ CHOISDEAILBH
nee Edith Drury
c. 1870-1950

When the Gaelic League was launched in 1894, its influence spread overseas and Edith Drury, born in London of Welsh and Irish parents, found herself in an environment where Irish dancing, Irish folk singing and

Kathleen Timoney.

the Irish language were treasured and revered.

She visited Aran and Dingle many times as a young girl, beginning at this early stage to jot down Irish melodies. Later she said it was her thirst for knowledge of Irish folk songs which motivated her.

As Edith's love grew for all things Gaelic and Irish, so too did her desire to live in Ireland. Even though becoming a Catholic meant resigning from her post as principal in St Michael's School, London, she did so. In 1902 she came to Ireland and took up a position as teacher in the Presentation Convent, Tuam, Galway. Here she met Dr Tom Costello and in 1903 was received into the catholic church, taking Eileen as her baptismal name. She married Tom and became known as Éibhlín Bean Uí Choisdeailbh.

During the next fifteen years Éibhlín continued her work of collecting folk songs. As she travelled the district, she would listen to people singing an air several times until she had completely captured it. She worked long, hard hours, but enjoyed every moment.

The Irish Folk Song Society of London offered to publish her book. In 1919 the Candle Press, Dawson Street, Dublin, printed *Amhráin Mhuigh Seola*, the majority of songs being collected from traditional singers in the Tuam district.

Éibhlín also helped in organising Feiseanna and Aeriocheachta in Tuam. She was instrumental in getting many of the local prize-winners to compete at the Oireachtas in Dublin.

MARY WESTBY
18th Century

Contract of employment for Mary Westby, the first recorded woman lighthouse keeper in Ireland. She was keeper of the Loop Head Lighthouse in County Clare and began work there on 18 March 1771. Her duties included the lighting of the fire there for the term of twenty one years after which time the contract ended.

JANE FRANCESCA: LADY WILDE 'SPERANZA' 1826-1896

Hating the 'brutality of strong lights', Francesca Wilde received no visitors until late afternoon, and even then, the shutters were drawn and dimmed lamps provided atmosphere.

There was nothing small or petty about Lady Wilde. In every way she lived on a large scale and, as with all people of strong and pronounced individuality, she inspired adoration or loathing. Her house in Merrion Square was the centre for those involved in the arts and sciences.

Born in Wexford in 1826, Jane Francesca Elgee was brought up in an atmosphere of intense conservatism. But, on reading a book entitled *The Spirit of the Nation*, her imagination blazed with poetry and patriotism.

In 1847, under the name of Speranza, she sent some poems to *The Nation*, a newspaper founded and edited by Gavan Duffy. Her work attracted much attention and most of her readers assumed her to be a man, including Gavan Duffy. Of these verses, hardly one has survived, although the few that do, along with her letters, reflect the glamour she trew over even the most mundane things.

One of her articles, 'Jacta Alea Est', led to the immediate suppression of the paper by the Government. Another, 'The Hour of Destiny', laid the author open to charges of high treason. During the trial of Gavan Duffy (he was accused of publishing seditious material in April 1849) these articles were a major source of controversy. Speranza instantly claimed the articles as her own.

As Speranza, she published a book of poems and as Lady Wilde, a number of works on folklore, and in 1854 she gave birth to a son, Oscar. The years modified her political opinions and, as she grew older, so she became mellower, running a fashionable salon in London, where she died on 3 February 1896.

MARGARET (PEG) WOFFINGTON 1714-1760

A wild and tempestuous spirit, together with a fine dramatic ability, made Peg Woffington one of the most exciting actresses of her day.

Her stormy career included numerous affairs and the spectacular stabbing in 1756 of her rival and compatriot, George Anne Bellamy. The public adored the notorious Peg, her vivacity

Know all Men by these presents That I, Mary Westby of the City of Dublin Widow am Holden & firmly bound unto our Sovereign Lord George the Third by the grace of God of Great Britain France and Ireland King defender of the faith in the sum of one thousand pounds Ster: to be paid unto our said Lord the King his Heirs or Successors for the true payment whereof I do hereby Bind me my Heirs Exors and Admors firmly by these presents Sealed with my Seal and dated this Eighteenth day of March one thousand seven hundred and Seventy one

Whereas by Indenture bearing even date herewith & made or mentioned to be made Between The Honble John Bourke Esq. ~ ~ ~ ~ ~ ~ ~ ~ ~ ~ ~ ~ ~ ~ ~ the Honble Bellingham Boyle Esqr. the Right Honble John Berresford The Right Honble Sir William Osborn Baronet Hugh Vallence Jones & John Milbank Esqrs Chief Commissrs and Governors of his Majestys Revenue in the Kingdom of Ireland for the present time being of the one part and the above bounden Mary Westby of the other part She the said Mary Westby was constituted and appointed Keeper the Lighthouse at Loophead at the Mouth of the River Shannon in the County of Clare And of the several Utinsills thereunto belonging & also lighter of the fire there to be kept for the Use & benefit of Shipping and Navigation To hold the said Office of Keeper of the said Light house & lighter of the Fire there to be kept unto the said Mary Westby her Exors & Admors from the First day of Novembr last past for the Term and Space of Twenty one years as by the said Indenture relation being thereunto had may more fully appear —

Now the Condition of the above obligation is such that if the above bounden Mary Westby her Exors & Admors do well truly perform fulfill and keep all & singular the Covenant Clauses & Agreements in the said Indenture mentioned & on part to be performed fulfilled & kept That then the above obligation shall be Void otherwise to remain in full force and Virtue in the law

Signed Sealed & delivered
in the presence of
Cha: Baldwell
C. Wm. Powe

M. Westby

Mary Westby's contract of employment.

and good humour counteracting what would otherwise be seen as intolerable behaviour.

In true Woffington style, she made her stage debut in a children's company at an amusement booth, conducted by the famous rope dancer, Madame Violante in George's Lane, Dublin. After playing a wide variety of roles in the Smock Alley Theatre, Dublin, she was offered an engagement in Covent Garden Theatre. Needless to say, she took London audiences by storm on her first appearance in November 1740. The following year she played in Drury Lane opposite David Garrick

and the two began a liaison which was to last for many years.

She maintained her connection with Dublin and in 1751, on her return, she was made president of the 'Beefsteak Club' — the *only* woman ever admitted to their weekly dinners. She returned to Covent Garden after three successful seasons in the Irish capital.

On 3 May 1757 she made her final appearance as Rosalind in *As You Like It*. She was taken ill on stage and soon retired from acting. On 28 March 1760 she died.

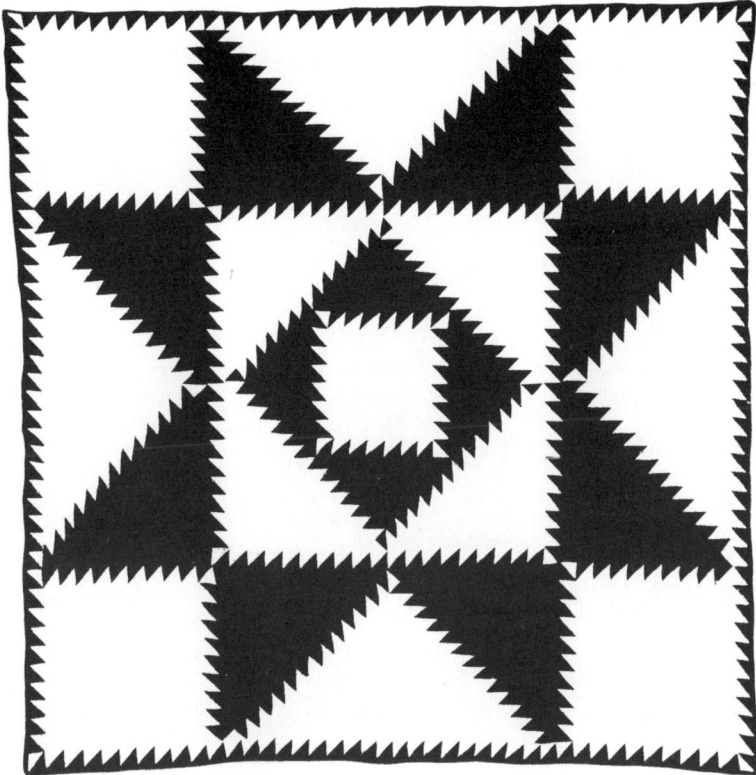

Patchwork. Ulster. 19th Century.

BIBLIOGRAPHY

ALLEN Mary — *Mary Anne McCracken* — Allen Figgis & Co. 1960

ANSCOMBE Isabelle — *Women in Design from 1860 to the Present Day* — Virago 1984

BARDON Jonathan — *Belfast An Illustrated History* — Blackstaff Press 1982

BEHAN Brian — *Mother of All the Behans An Autobiography of Kathleen Behan as told to Brian Behan* — Hutchinson 1984

BLEAKLEY David — *Saidie Patterson, Irish Peacemaker* — Blackstaff Press, 1980

BOYLAN H — *A Dictionary of Irish Biography* — Gill & Macmillan 1978

CASEY Elizabeth Blackburne E. Owens — *Illustrious Irish Women from the earliest ages to the present day* — Tinsley 1877

CONCANNON Mrs Helena — *Women of '98* — Dublin, Gill 1919

CONLON JF — *Some Irish Poets and Musicians*

CRONE John S — *A Concise Dictionary of Irish Biography* — Talbot Press 1928

DID YOUR GRANNY HAVE A HAMMER??? — *A History of the Irish Suffrage Movement 1876-1922* — Attic Press 1985

FOX RM — *Rebel Irishwomen* — Progress House 1935

FLYNN Elizabeth Gurley — *I Speak My Own Piece; Autobiography of the Rebel Girl* — New York, Masses & Mainstream 1955

HAMILTON CJ — *Notable Irishwomen* — Sealy Bryers & Walker Dublin

HOLLAND Vyvyan — *Oscar Wilde and his World* — Thames & Hudson 1978

IRELAND John de Courcy — *Wrecks and Rescue off the East Coast* — Glendale Press 1983

IRELAND OF THE WELCOMES — May/June 1982

IRISH PATCHWORK: — Assembled by Alex Meldrum Introduction by Laura Jones — Sponsors AIB Kilkenny Design Workshops Ltd 1979

MISSING PIECES — *Women in Irish History Since the Famine* — Irish Feminist Information/Attic Press 1984

MACKSEY Joan & Kenneth — *The Guinness Guide to Feminine Achievements* — Guinness Superlatives Ltd. 1975

McTERNAN John *MODERN IRISH* *LANDSCAPE* *PAINTING*	*Here's To Their Memory* *Irish Art Series No. 1*	Mercier Press 1977 Dublin, The Arts Councils in Ireland 1981
MOLLOY J. Fitzgerald	*The Romance of the Irish* *Stage.*	London
O'CONLUAIN	*Islands and Authors*	Mercier Press 1983
O'HARA Bernard ed	*Mayo: Aspects of its Heritage*	Galway: Archaeological Historical & Folklore Society, Regional Technical College, 1982
O'HARE Aidan	*A Tribute to Delia Murphy*	Connaught Telegraph 1982
O'LAOI Padraig	*Nora Barnacle: A Portrait*	Galway: Kenny's Bookshops and Art Galleries 1982
O'NEILL Capt. Francis	*Irish Minstrels and Musicians*	Chicago: Regan Gallerie 1913
O'SÚILLEABHÁIN Sean	*Longford Authors*	Mullingar: Longford/ Westmeath Joint Library Committee 1978
O'TUAMA Séan Kinsella Thomas	*An Duanaire:* *Poems of the Dispossessed*	Dolmen Press 1981
OWENS Rosemary Cullen	*Smashing Times:* *A History of the Irish Women's* *Suffrage Movement 1889-1922*	Attic Press 1984
PETERSEN Karen WILSON JJ	*Women Artists: Recognition* *and Reappraisal from the Early* *Ages to the Twentieth Century*	The Women's Press 1978
ROSCOMMON YEAR *BOOK 1984*		
SIMPSON Janet Madden	*Woman's Part: An Anthology* *of Short Fiction by and about* *Irishwomen 1890-1960*	Arlen House 1984
SÍNSEAR	An Cumann Bealoideas Eireann 1982/83 & 1980/81	
THOM A	*Thom's Irish Who's Who*	Dublin 1923
VAN VORIS Jaqueline	*Constance de Markievicz:* *In the Cause of Ireland*	Amherst: University of Massachussetts Press 1967
WEBB Alfred	*Compendium of Irish Biography*	MH Gill 1878

MISSING PIECES — SUBJECT INDEX

Crow, Eileen 46
Cranwill, Mia 17
Cumann na mBan 19, 20, 23, 32, 44, 51
Cumann na nGaedhl 20
Curran, Sarah 18
Curran, Gertrude 18
Dancer 40
Deevey, Teresa 19
de Meath, Petronilla 31
Dempsey, Kate 20
Derry 28
Designer 17, 26
de Valera, Eamonn 23
de Valera, Maírín 20
Dockrell, Margaret Sarah 21
Dolmen Press 18
Dominican Convent 38, 48
Donegal 11, 40, 46
Drury, Edith 52
Dublin 12, 13, 15, 18, 19, 21, 24, 32, 40, 42, 46, 49, 50
Duncan, Ellen 21
Early, Biddy 38
Edgeworth, Maria 37
Elvery, Beatrice 46
Emmet, Robert 19
Farrell MJ see Molly Keane 46
Farren, Elizabeth 22
Fermanagh 33
Flanagan, Elizabeth 23
Flynn, Elizabeth Gurley 23
France 21, 26, 27, 28, 30, 49, 50

Francis, ME 24
Fry, Elizabeth 34
Furlong, Jack 12
Gaelic League 52
Gallagher, Beezie, 24
Galway 9, 40, 51
Garrick, David 13, 26, 55
Germany 11, 32
Gonne McBride, Maud 12, 17
Gray, Eileen 26
Gregory, Lady 17
Gunning, Elizabeth 13, 22, 26
Gunning, Maria 17, 13
Gunning, Maria 26

MORE AND MORE MISSING PIECES . . .

More Missing Pieces is the second in a series designed to reclaim forgotten women and replace them in our her story books. Research shows that there are hundreds of women who deserve inclusion. You can help compile a third edition by getting information on those women you would like to have remembered.

Sources of information are your local libraries; historical societies; local folklore/oral history; parish records; National Library of Ireland. Photo research can be done through the national or provincial newspapers.

INFORMATION NEEDED

NAME:

PLACE OF BIRTH:

DATE OF BIRTH:

OCCUPATION:

ANECDOTES:

ILLUSTRATION/PHOTOGRAPH:

SOURCE:

Then, send your
information to
Attic Press,
48, Fleet Street,
Dublin 2.